The Lemonade Babysitter

by Karen Waggoner

Pictures by Dorothy Donohue

Little, Brown and Company

Boston   Toronto   London

First Edition

Library of Congress Cataloging-in-Publication Data

Waggoner, Karen.
    The lemonade babysitter / by Karen Waggoner ; pictures by Dorothy Donohue. — 1st ed.
        p.   cm.
    Summary: Molly thinks she can take care of herself, so when old Mr. Herbert comes to babysit, she uses all her resources to try to discourage him from ever coming back.
    ISBN 0-316-91711-7
    [1. Babysitters — Fiction.   2. Old age — Fiction.]   I. Donohue, Dorothy, ill.   II. Title.
PZ7.W12413Le   1992
[E] — dc20   91-32915

10 9 8 7 6 5 4 3 2

WOR

Published simultaneously in Canada
by Little, Brown & Company (Canada) Limited

Printed in the United States of America

To Gene and Wini, with love

— K. W.

In memory of my dad

— D. D.

"No more babysitters!" Molly told her mother when the doorbell rang. "I'm going to your office with you!"

Molly had gone there yesterday after her babysitter quit. She had sharpened pencils and washed coffee cups, licked stamps, and drawn pictures to hang on the walls. At the end of the day, everyone had told Molly what a big helper she was.

"Thank you very much," she'd said. "See you tomorrow!"

The doorbell rang again. "Just open the door, Molly," said her mother. "It's a surprise."

Molly peeked out. It was only old Mr. Herbert from down the street. He had on the same rumpled sweater and polka dot bow tie he always wore. Maybe he was looking for his old gray cat.

"How do?" Mr. Herbert said. "I'm your new babysitter."

"I don't need a babysitter!" Molly declared. "I'm too big."

"I'm glad to hear that, because I've never babysat before," Mr. Herbert said. He made his tangly eyebrows bounce. "You'll have to teach me what babysitters do."

Molly wound her hair around her finger. Maybe she could think of things Mr. Herbert would never want to do. Then he'd quit, and she could go to her mother's office again.

"Okay," she agreed.

By the time her mother had hugged her and said good-bye, Molly knew just what to tell Mr. Herbert.

"The first thing babysitters do," she said, "is let me fix their hair."

Mr. Herbert bent way over and patted the bald top of his head. "That won't take long."

But Molly made it take forever. She spritzed Mr. Herbert's hair with water and made it stand straight up in the air. On top, she drew a smiley face with lipstick. Surely that would make him mad.

It didn't.

She wiped his head and drew a frown.

"I must look very handsome by now," was all he said.

Molly turned on the radio. "Babysitters let me give them dancing lessons. Watch what I can do."

She skipped and stomped and twirled until she toppled
on the couch.

"My turn," said Mr. Herbert as he changed the station. "I can 'Shuffle Off to Buffalo.'" He straightened his bow tie and began.

From the knees up it didn't look like dancing, but his feet whisked back and forth like little brooms. Mr. Herbert danced much better than Molly's last babysitter. But Molly still didn't want *any* babysitter. She hoped Mr. Herbert would get so tired he'd never come back.

"I could do this forever," he said, shuffling around the room.

Molly didn't say a word during lunch. She was trying to think of something Mr. Herbert would never *ever* want to do.

"After lunch, babysitters take me to the zoo," she said at last. The zoo was almost as much fun as her mother's office, but baby-sitters never wanted to take her there.

"The zoo? Haven't been there in years," Mr. Herbert said with a frown. "But I betcha I can find it!"

Molly and Mr. Herbert had to catch two buses. She paid half fare because she was so young. He paid half fare because he was so old.

It was a long ride. While Mr. Herbert looked out the window, Molly made plans.

When they stepped off the bus, Molly said, "Babysitters always take me on the zoo train." She was sure Mr. Herbert's long legs wouldn't fit.

But he folded himself next to her inside the last car. The train chugged past giraffes and elephants, rhinos and hippos, lions and tigers and bears.

"Lions and tigers and bears!" Molly chanted.

Mr. Herbert chanted, too. "Lions and tigers and bears!"

In the tunnel, Molly went, "WOOO-ooo-OOOOOO!"

A lady covered her ears. But Mr. Herbert sang out,

"WOOO-ooo-OOOOOOO!" even louder.

"Next stop snack bar," Mr. Herbert said. "If that's what baby-sitters do."

Molly thought that was a good idea, but she didn't say so. "My mother doesn't let me eat hot dogs," she warned.

Mr. Herbert patted his stomach. "Doc says I can't have them either. Now, lemonade would hit the spot."

But the lemonade stand was closed. "Candy apples?" Molly asked.

"Nope. False teeth"

"I've got a loose tooth," Molly said and wiggled it for him. "A candy apple might make it come out too soon."

"Yogurt pops!" they decided, then watched the seals catch fish.

At the gift shop Molly said, "Babysitters and I always try on funny hats. You be a giraffe. I'll be a tiger."

"How do, Missy Tiger?" Mr. Herbert said, making his eyebrows bounce.

"How do, Mr. Giraffe?" said Molly.

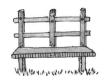

On the way back to the bus, they watched the macaques play.

"Those monkeys come from Japan," Mr. Herbert told her. "That's a long ways away."

"My dad lives in Oregon," Molly said. "That's really a long ways away."

"Well, now. My daughter's in Arizona. That's just as far, and it costs so much to fly there, I see her only once a year."

Molly stuck out her chin. "My best friend moved to Altoona, and I never *ever* get to see her at all."

"You don't say. . . ." Mr. Herbert shook his head.

"At least you have your old gray cat," Molly said.

"Nope. She died last month. We were friends a long time."

"Oh. Best friends?"

"The very best."

Molly was quiet. Just before the bus pulled up, she took Mr. Herbert's hand.

"Your hand is very sticky," he said.

"Maybe *your* hand is sticky," Molly replied.

When they got home, Molly tugged Mr. Herbert into the playroom. "Want to see my animals?" she asked. If Mr. Herbert liked the zoo, he would love Brownbear, Kimmie Cat, and Pippin, Poppin, and Mumby.

Mr. Herbert sank deep into the chair, leaned against Brownbear, and closed his eyes. "I'll never be able to get up," he said.

"Here's Wobbles," Molly said, tucking her rabbit under Mr. Herbert's arm. "She's good to hug."

Mr. Herbert smiled at Wobbles and sighed.

Molly knew what else Mr. Herbert would like. "I'll be right back," she said and ran to the kitchen.

There was only one lemon left. Molly rolled it to make it extra juicy. She squeezed the lemon into two glasses, then added water, sugar, and ice.

At the playroom door, she peeked in. Mr. Herbert hadn't
budged.

"How do?" she said and made her eyebrows bounce. "Let's have lemonade!"

"Oh, ho!" he said. "Is that what babysitters do?"

Molly grinned. "Yes," she said, "that's what babysitters do."

The Lemonade
Babysitter